LITTLE MISS CHATTERBOX
and the Frog Prince
Roger Hargreaves

Original concept by
Roger Hargreaves

Written and illustrated by
Adam Hargreaves

EGMONT

D0353871

It will come as no surprise to you to hear that Little Miss Chatterbox likes to chatter.

She will chatter all day long.

Non stop, incessantly, without a pause, until the cows come home …

… go to bed …

… and wake up the next morning.

And it will also come as no surprise to you to hear that all this chattering gets on people's nerves.

Particularly some people.

People like Little Miss Bossy, who got cornered by Little Miss Chatterbox outside the post office.

"Good morning, Little Miss Bossy," started Little Miss Chatterbox. "Although good is probably not really the right description with all this rain we've been having and actually we're getting wet standing around chatting in the rain like this but it was so nice to see you that I thought I must stop and say 'Good morning' although as I just said good is not really …"

"Oh, do be quiet!" cried Little Miss Bossy, and she stomped off down the street.

And impatient people like Mr Rude, who got caught behind Little Miss Chatterbox in a queue at the butcher's.

"I must say Mr Chop that this is a wonderful display of meat," she said to the butcher. "It must take you a very long time to prepare it all. What time do you get up in the morning? It must be very early. I get up quite early but you must get up even earlier. I bet you have sausages in the morning for breakfast. I have a bowl of…"

"Who cares!" shouted Mr Rude and he stormed out of the shop.

Poor Little Miss Chatterbox.

It is not very nice to be shouted at just when you think you are enjoying a polite conversation with somebody.

Sometimes it makes Little Miss Chatterbox feel very sad, and one of those times she went for a walk in the woods.

As she walked along, talking to herself, she came to a pond where she saw a frog sitting on a lily pad, so she sat down for a rest.

"Well, Mr Frog, you have a lovely spot here in the sun. It must be nice being a frog and not having everybody tell you to be quiet," she said to the frog. "Nobody else wants to listen to me so I might as well talk to you."

And so she did.

She talked for hours to the frog.

She poured her heart out.

Poor Little Miss Chatterbox.

And all the while, the frog sat very still on his lily pad, watching her.

Finally, Little Miss Chatterbox paused for a breath.

"Well, that's a terribly sad tale," said the frog.

Said the frog!

The frog could speak!

Little Miss Chatterbox could not believe her ears.

"Well I never," said Little Miss Chatterbox.
"A talking frog."

The frog beamed. "It's good to have someone so interesting to talk to," he said.

The frog and Little Miss Chatterbox had a wonderful conversation. They talked about everything and anything until it was time for Little Miss Chatterbox to go home.

"Could I come back tomorrow?" asked Little Miss Chatterbox.

"That would be lovely," replied the frog.

And she did go back the next day.

And the day after that.

And even the day after that.

In fact, she went back every day for the next week.

Then one day, Little Miss Chatterbox said, "You are such a good listener, I could kiss you."

And without saying another word, she did.

She kissed the frog!

And then something utterly remarkable happened.

With a clap of thunder and in a cloud of smoke, the frog magically turned into a prince.

For the first time in her life, Little Miss Chatterbox was lost for words.

"Thank you!" cried the prince. "A bad wizard turned me into a frog when I was young because I wouldn't stop talking and only a freely-given kiss could break the spell!"

The prince then took Little Miss Chatterbox to his kingdom, where everybody welcomed him back with open arms.

And the prince was so grateful that he gave Little Miss Chatterbox a job at the palace.

She is now the Official Royal Chatterer on the palace radio station!